SMYTHE GAMBRELL LIBRARY
USA
USA
USA
WESTMINSTER SCHOOLS
1982
PRESENTED BY
Kristen Holloway

THE GOOSE AND THE GOLDEN COINS

also retold and illustrated by Lorinda Bryan Cauley
THE UGLY DUCKLING

also illustrated by Lorinda Bryan Cauley
CURLEY CAT BABY-SITS by Pauline Watson
THE WAR PARTY by William O. Steele
BILL PICKETT: *First Black Rodeo Star* by Sibyl Hancock
OLD HIPPO'S EASTER EGG by Jan Wahl

THE GOOSE AND THE GOLDEN COINS

Retold and illustrated by Lorinda Bryan Cauley

HARCOURT BRACE JOVANOVICH NEW YORK AND LONDON

Requests for permission to make copies of any part of the work should be mailed to: Permissions, Harcourt Brace Jovanovich, Inc., 757 Third Avenue, New York, New York 10017.

Printed in the United States of America

LIBRARY OF CONGRESS CATALOGING IN PUBLICATION DATA

Cauley, Lorinda Bryan.
The goose and the golden coins.
A retelling of the folktale L'oca
from Il pentamerone by G. B. Basile.
SUMMARY: Retells the tale of the goose
that dropped golden coins.
[1. Folklore—Italy]
I. Basile, Giovanni Battista, 1575 (ca.)–1632.
Pentamerone. Oca. II. Title.
PZ8.1.C25Go [398.2] [E] 80-24591
ISBN 0-15-232206-X ISBN 0-15-232207-8 (pbk.)

B C D E FIRST EDITION B C D E (PBK.)

HBJ

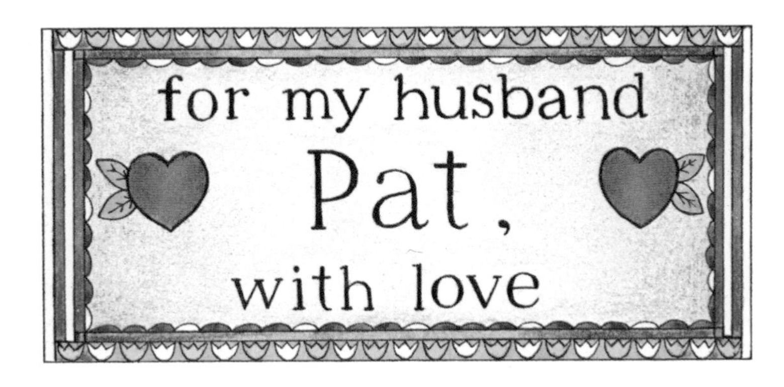
for my husband
Pat,
with love

THE ORIGIN OF THE TALE

It wasn't until the seventeenth century that the first great collection of folktales, previously handed down by word of mouth, gathering greater embellishments with each new telling, was actually set down by Giambattista Basile in the Neapolitan dialect. Basile's prose was witty and animated, in the often bawdy spirit of his people.

In reading his candid narrations of these tales (which include the earliest versions of Cinderella, Puss in Boots, Rapunzel, and other familiar stories), I was drawn to Basile's exuberant, light-hearted version of "The Goose," which is surely the ancestor of today's more refined "The Goose That Laid the Golden Egg."

The original struck me as being refreshingly frank and human, with the kind of unadorned and blatant humor young children love. Wanting to share it with them, I have created my own version by slightly altering that of Basile's, but making a great effort to preserve the vitality of his prose and his robust humor.

Lorinda Bryan Cauley

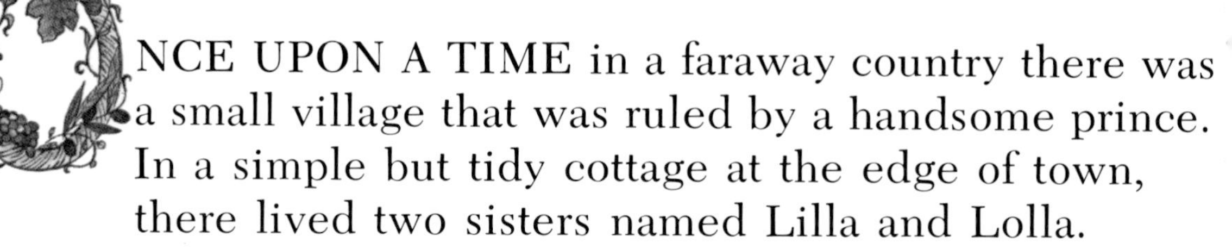

ONCE UPON A TIME in a faraway country there was a small village that was ruled by a handsome prince. In a simple but tidy cottage at the edge of town, there lived two sisters named Lilla and Lolla.

The sisters were very poor and had to spin flax from morning until evening just in order to eat. When they had spun enough flax, they would take it to the market to sell.

Then with their hard-earned money they would buy some potatoes and cabbage and a bit of marrowbone.

These they would take home to make a large pot of soup. It would have to last the week through, until they had enough flax to sell again.

And so their life dragged on day after day, week after week, until one morning, when they were at the market, their eyes fell upon a goose for sale that was tethered in a most cruel way.

The gentle hearts of the maidens were touched by the poor bird's plight, and instead of buying the usual vegetables, they bought the goose instead.

Lilla and Lolla put the goose in their basket and carried her down the road that led to their cottage.

They made her feel quite at home and fed her plenty of broth and bread. The goose was allowed to sleep in their own bed and was loved as if she were a sister.

The days passed, and the sisters kept busy as usual, spinning, marketing, cooking, and cleaning. But the presence of the goose brought them an extra feeling of joy.

One day, to the astonishment of all, instead of natural droppings, the goose began to drop golden coins! It wasn't long before there were enough gold coins to fill a large chest.

Now the sisters had enough money to buy dresses made of fine linens and lace. They wore fancy hats and dainty shoes, and when they went out, they began to lift their heads with pride.

At the market they bought the richest of foods, prime cuts of meat and delicate pastries. The gossips in the town began to take notice of their sudden wealth and were filled with envy and curiosity.

One evening the gossips went to the sisters' cottage and began to spy on them.

They watched as Lilla and Lolla spread a sheet on the floor and coaxed the goose to walk across it. As she did, she began dropping golden coins. The sisters gathered up the coins and put them into a chest.

The next morning one of the gossips came to visit the sisters at their home. She told them that she needed to borrow the goose to hatch some motherless gosling eggs. Partly out of kindness and partly not to cause suspicion, the sisters agreed to lend the goose. The gossip promised to return her as soon as the eggs were hatched.

The gossip took the goose to her home, where the others eagerly awaited her. They laid clean sheets upon the floor and roughly forced the goose to walk on them. But to their dismay, instead of golden coins, there came only droppings in their natural state.

When they saw such a sight, they decided they should feed her special food that would turn the droppings into gold. So they gathered together a feast fit for a king and pushed the food down the poor goose's throat.

But this time indigestion only made matters worse. The gossips became so disgusted that they twisted the goose's neck until they thought she was dead. Then they threw her out of the window into a passageway.

About the same time the prince and his servants arrived, and the prince, on a matter of important business, walked into the passageway.

Now the goose was *not* dead but filled with great anger at her treatment. Turning her head, she caught sight of the prince as he passed by, and biting him from behind, she refused to let go.

He cried in agony for his servants' aid. They pulled and tugged, but it was of no help. The goose held fast to her booty.

Finally the prince ordered his men to carry him to the palace.

There he sent for all the doctors and sages of his realm to find a way to loosen the goose's hold. They tried ointments and powders of all kinds. They even made use of pinchers, but nothing worked.

Realizing that the goose was like a tick that would not let go, he issued a proclamation. "Whosoever shall deliver me from this annoyance, if it should be a man, I will give him half my realm; if a woman, I will take her to be my wife."

The townsfolk, hearing of the reward, swarmed to the palace gate with remedies of every sort.

Some tried to entice her with fake mating calls, and even real live ganders, but she would not be lured.

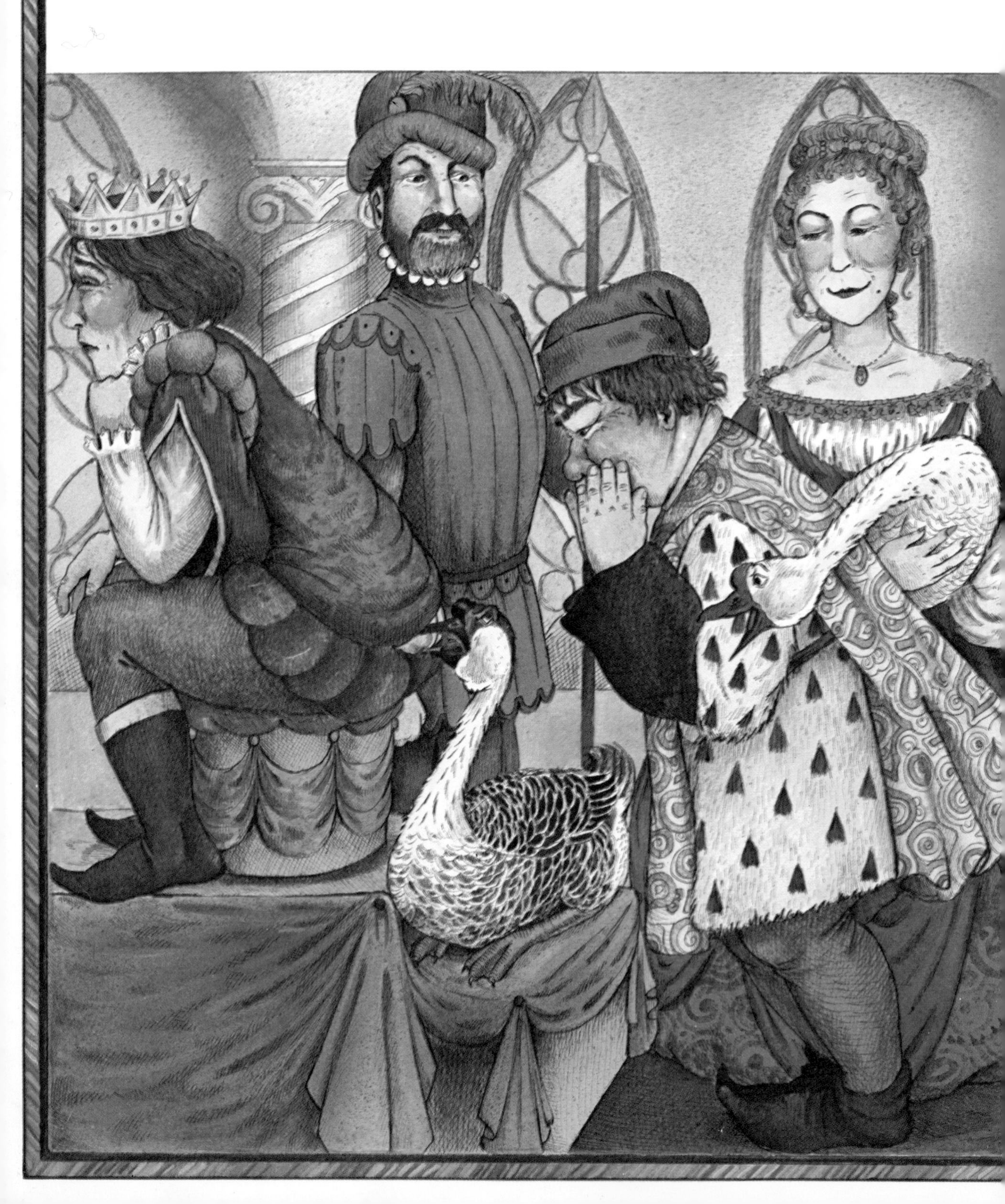

Others tried to distract her with juggling and magic acts, or to induce her to sleep with lullabies.

Still others attempted to frighten her.

Delectable dishes were offered to her, but all of these things only made her more determined to hold on.

Finally, among all who came and went, came Lolla, the younger of the two sisters. When she saw the goose, she realized she knew her and let out a cry of joy.

The goose, hearing the voice of her beloved mistress, at once let go and ran to meet her.

The prince, seeing this marvel, asked how it could have happened. So Lolla told the story from the beginning to the end. When she came to the part where the goose played the trick on the gossips, the prince laughed until he fell backward.

Then he commanded that the gossips be placed in the town stocks for all to see.

After that, amid much joy and feasting, he took Lolla for his wife and, for her dowry, the goose that could drop so many treasures.

And soon after, he married her sister Lilla
to a duke, and they all lived happily ever after.